This Walker book
belongs to:

....

....

....

Let's Go to

Caryl Hart

Bee and Billy,

Billy and Bee,

See what they

can do!

WALKER BOOKS
AND SUBSIDIARIES
LONDON · BOSTON · SYDNEY · AUCKLAND

For Jess, with love, Mum xx≈C.H. ▾▴▾ To Oscar George Viney≈L.T. ◆ First published 2018 by Walker Books Ltd, 87 Vauxhall Walk, London SE11 5HJ
This edition published 2019 ◆ Text © 2018 Caryl Hart ◆ Illustrations © 2018 Lauren Tobia ◆ The right of Caryl Hart and Lauren Tobia to be
identified as author and illustrator respectively of this work has been asserted by them in accordance with the Copyright, Designs and Patents Act 1988

the Seaside!

Lauren Tobia

They're so
tumbly,
wiggly,
jumbly!
Can YOU
do it, too?

Bare toes scrunch
in crunchy sand,
Children run
and play.
Look, it's Bee
and Billy...

They're on the **BEACH!** Hooray!

White sand meets the big blue sea,

Blue sea meets the sky.

"WOW!" cries Bee.

"An orange kite, dancing way up high!"

Let's spread the picnic blanket,

Unpack buckets, spades and hats.

Climb into sunsuits, zippedy-zip!

Gloopy sunscreen splats!

Bee shouts, **"I want to paddle!"**

She runs across the sand.

"Wait for me!" cries Billy.

"Come on, Billy! Hold my hand!"

Foamy waves swoosh up the beach,

TUMBLE RUMBLE SPLASH!

Bee wiggles, giggles,

"Can't catch me!"

Ready steady ... wave dash!

Then SPLOSH!
A giant wave
sneaks up.
It takes Bee
by surprise.

"Help!" wails Bee. "It's freezing!

The sea's gone in my eyes!"

"Whoops!" smiles Mummy. "You're OK."

Bee sobs, "I HATE the sea!

It's salty, wet and NAUGHTY!"

Billy shrugs, "It's nice!

Look, Bee!"

Snuggled up in fluffy towels,

They warm up in the sun.

There's hot chocolate and a picnic,

MUNCH CRUNCH everyone!

Bee finds her orange bucket,

And sits down in the shade.

Shovel sand in.

Pat it flat.

"Look what we have made!"

"Let's use these shells for windows.

This stone can be the door."

Can Billy count them?

Yes he can!

"One, two, three,

FOUR!"

Sandy shoulders, knees and toes,

Hair stiff from salt and sun.

Here's Mummy with a lovely treat,

Ice creams for EVERYONE!

A chilly wind blows off the sea,

The sun begins to set.

"Time to pack," says Mummy.

Bee is cross. **"We can't go YET!"**

Billy shares the picnic crusts,

Seagulls swoop and screech.

"Goodbye gulls!"

shouts Bee.

"We LOVE it on the beach!"

Bee and Billy
are going
home,
Today has
been
such fun.

They're yawny,

sleepy,

snuggly,

tired...

Goodbye, everyone!

Also illustrated by Lauren Tobia:

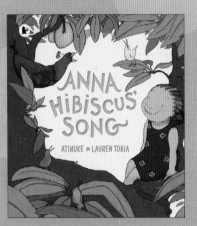

978-1-4063-3841-6

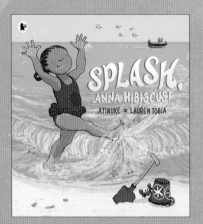

978-1-4063-5468-3

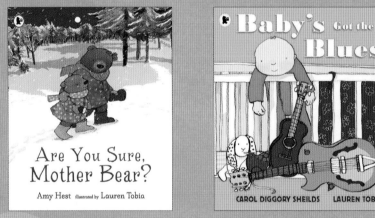

978-1-4063-7807-8

978-1-4063-6004-2

Caryl Hart is the author of more than thirty books for children.
She lives in Sheffield with her husband and two daughters.
Find her online at **carylhart.com** and on Twitter as **@carylhart1**.

Lauren Tobia lives in Bristol with her husband and their two Jack Russell terriers, Poppy and Tilly.
Find her online at **laurentobia.com** and on Twitter and Instagram as **@laurentobia**.

Available from all good booksellers

www.walker.co.uk